8-1

Why
a Donkey
was Chosen

To my children
Anna
and
Rachel
and my Godchildren
Megan
Michael
ChiChi
and
Nigel

By CHRISTOPHER GREGOROWSKI

Library of Congress Catalog Card No. 75-24951
Text copyright © 1975 by Christopher Gregorowski
Illustrations copyright © 1975 by Ernest Benn Ltd.
First edition in the United States of America
Second impression 1978
Printed photolitho in Great Britain by
Ebenezer Baylis & Son Ltd., The Trinity Press,
Worcester, and London

ISBN 0-385-11569-5 TRADE
0-385-14414-8 PREBOUND

GARDEN CITY, NEW YORK

a Donkey was Chosen

Illustrated by CAROLINE BROWNE

DOUBLEDAY & COMPANY INC.

One day, Reuben was walking
down the road.
He was thinking
about nothing in particular
when he saw a notice on a wall.
So he went closer, to read it.

Funny notice.
It must be in
Arabic
or Hebrew
or
¡uʍop ǝpᴉsdn

Wanted:
Elephants, Camels,
Horses, Dromedaries,
Llamas, Oxen,
but not Donkeys.

Not wanted
Donkeys.
Why not Donkeys?

We Donkeys have
lovely ears
but they are nothing
like an Elephant's
ears

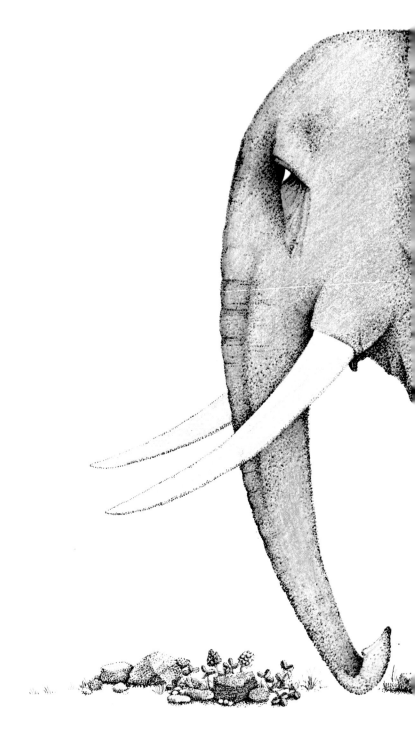

and we have no
trunk
or tusks

strange if we had . . .

9

We Donkeys have
lovely eyes
but they are nothing
like a Camel's eyes

and we have no humps

strange if we had . . .

11

We Donkeys are very
strong
but not as strong as
an Ox

and we have no horns
like those of an Ox

strange
if we had . . .

14

So Donkeys are not
wanted to carry
important people,
only little people.
So I won't apply here
will I?

So, while the Elephants
Camels, Horses,
Dromedaries, Llamas,
Oxen went to
apply here,

Reuben went to eat
some grass.

And while the
Elephant was sent
to India to carry
the Rajah

and the Camel

was sent to Egypt

to carry

the Pharoah

and the Horse
was sent to Rome
to carry
the Caesar

and the Dromedary,
Llama and Ox were
sent elsewhere
to carry
Kings and Sheiks
and the Shahs and
the Queens and the
Emperors and
Sultans and
Tetrarchs,

Reuben stayed at home
and ate grass
and waited for someone to
carry . . .

24

. . . a little person, perhaps.

25

And then a man came along and saw Reuben and spoke to him.
"I am looking for a beast of burden to carry an Important Person."

But Reuben shook his head
and said:
"All the beasts of burden
who carry important people
have gone far away."

"I am a donkey.
Donkeys are not wanted
to carry
important people.

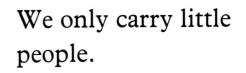

We only carry little
people.

Do you see?
. . . Donkeys cannot
be too proud."

"I am proud of my ears
but they are nothing like
an Elephant's ears."

I am proud of my eyes
but they are nothing like
a Camel's eyes."

"So I have much to be proud of.
But not too proud.
I have no trunk or tusks
or hump or horns.

Imagine me if I had!"

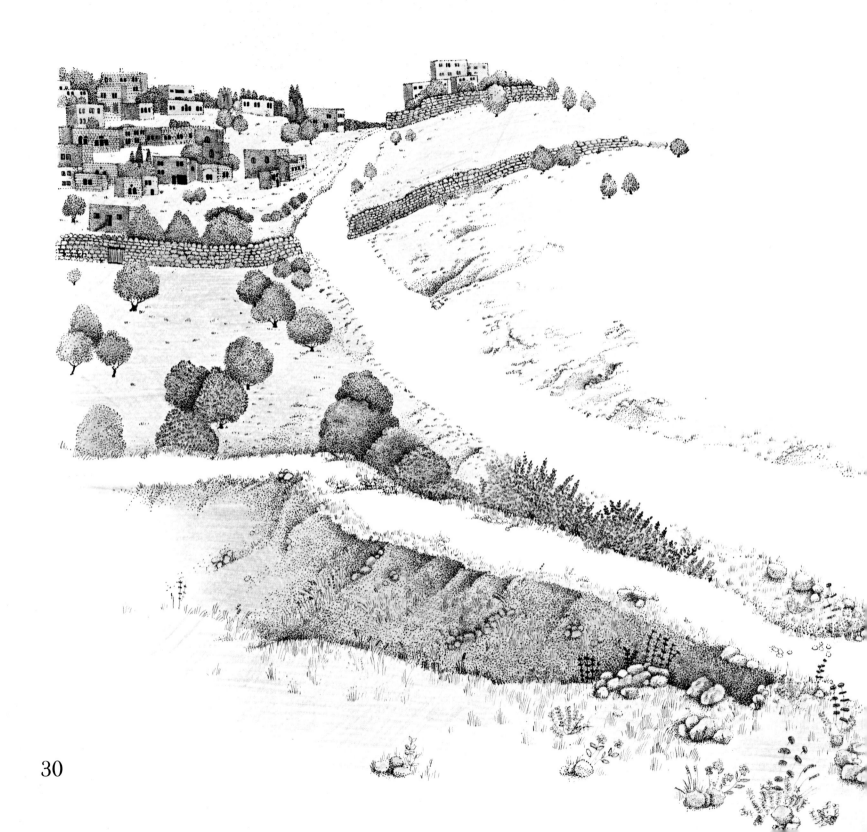

The man laughed,
and then he said:
"This Important Person
is also a very little person,
for he is an unborn child.
He is the Messiah and his
name is Jesus."

"His mother needs to be
carried by a beast
of burden who cannot
be too proud,
so I have chosen you,
a donkey, to carry her to
Bethlehem where her son
will be born."